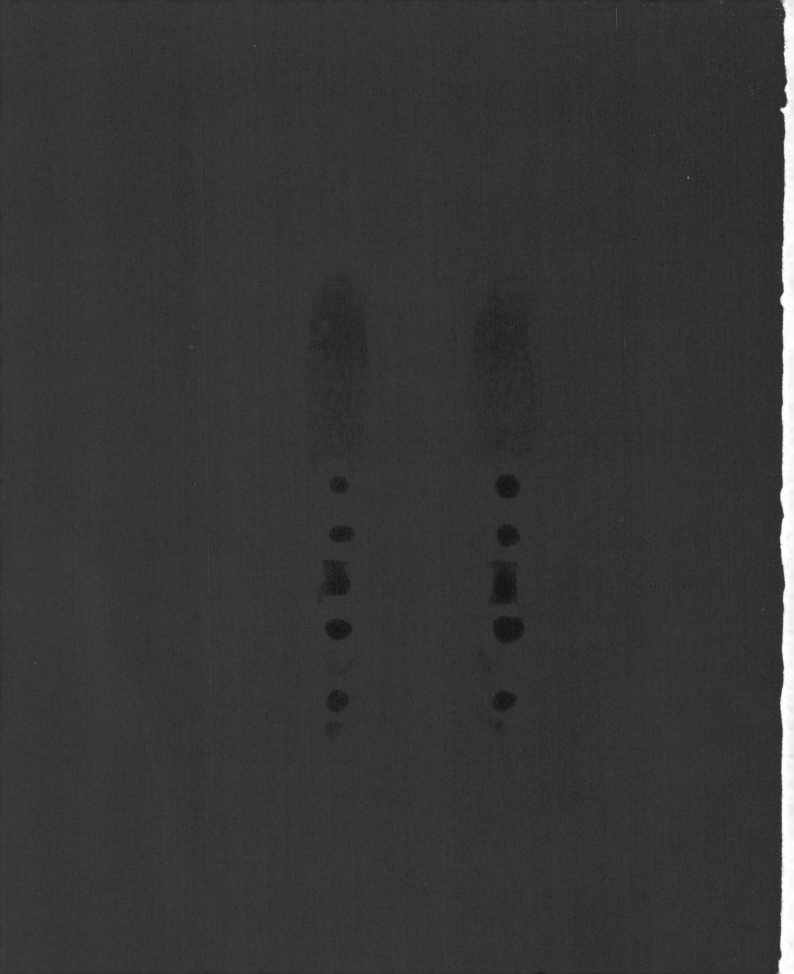

Extraordinary Eyes

How Animals See the World

Extraordinary Eyes

How Animals See the World

by **Sandra Sinclair**

Dial Books for Young Readers *New York*

For Candace

Published by Dial Books for Young Readers
A Division of Penguin Books USA Inc.
375 Hudson Street
New York, New York 10014

Copyright © 1992 by Sandra Sinclair
Printed in Hong Kong
Design by Nancy R. Leo
First Edition
1 2 3 4 5 6 7 8 9 10

Library of Congress Cataloging in Publication Data

Sinclair, Sandra.
Extraordinary eyes : how animals see the world / by Sandra Sinclair.
p. cm.
Summary: Describes how vision works, and compares
and contrasts the eyes of such animals as
the honeybee, fish, frog, and bird.
ISBN 0-8037-0803-3.—ISBN 0-8037-0806-8 (lib. bdg.)
1. Vision—Juvenile literature. 2. Animals—Juvenile literature.
[1. Vision. 2. Animals—Sense organs.] I. Title.
QP475.7.S565 1992 591.1'823—dc20 89-39618 CIP AC

✻ Table of Contents

*E*yes don't always come in simple pairs. There are animals with clusters of eyes, others with eyes at the end of tentacles, and even animals with eyes in their feet. Many animals see better than we do. The hawk and the eagle see farther than we can. Butterflies and birds see more colors. Raccoons, cats, and owls see well at night, when we are almost blind in dim light. Some snakes, in addition to their normal eyes, have sensors that make images out of heat radiation and can "see" in pitch blackness. Animals we might consider primitive, like bacteria, beetles, and many deep-sea creatures, can even create their own light to attract or signal other animals. Eyes are one of nature's most extraordinary creations.

Up close the damsel fly, with its large compound eyes, appears almost like a creature from another planet. Jack Drafahl–IMAGE CONCEPTS

The single-lens eye of this young golden eagle sees much farther than our own single-lens eye. Len Rue, Jr.

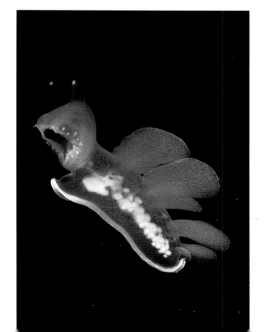

The lion nutabranch, a tiny marine creature, glows with bioluminescent light. Jack Drafahl–IMAGE CONCEPTS

1

1 ❧ A Backbone Makes a Difference

The first scientists who studied animal life divided the animal kingdom into two kinds: animals that have backbones and an internal skeleton that supports the body, and animals that do not. Animals with backbones are called *vertebrates* (**ver**-teh-brits). These include all mammals (the group to which humans belong), as well as fish, birds, reptiles, and amphibians.

Any animal without a backbone and an internal skeleton was more or less lumped together in a larger group known as *invertebrates* (**in-ver**-teh-brits). The invertebrate group includes all animals with soft bodies, like worms and octopuses; hard exterior shells, like clams and snails, which are called *mollusks;* soft shells, like crabs and lobsters, called *crustaceans* (krus-**tay**-she-uns); and the huge group of insects.

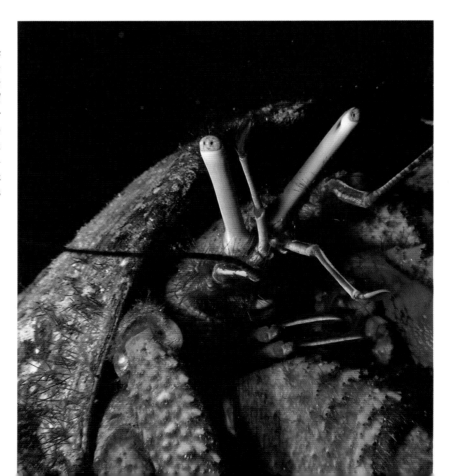

A hermit crab's eyes are like periscopes that can be extended outside or pulled back into its shell. Jack Drafahl– IMAGE CONCEPTS

2

Only recently have we learned that another major difference separates vertebrates from invertebrates—the origin of their eyes. The eyes of all invertebrates evolved from a part of the skin. This fact may account for the unusual locations of eyes in some primitive invertebrates. For example, the eyes of the queen conch are found at the ends of its tentacles, and the starfish has eyes

Two bat starfish stare at one another. Starfish eyes are found in their feet, which means that they must step quite carefully. Jack Drafahl —Image Concepts

on its feet. However, unlike its other senses, the eye of the vertebrate animal is a *direct outgrowth of its brain.* As animals evolve, this eye–brain connection becomes more important.

2 ❧ How Eyes Work

The first living creatures on earth had no eyes at all—just small clumps of cells that were sensitive to light. We call them *eyespots* and they are still found in many small, soft-skinned creatures such as earthworms. Eyespots detect light, which helps a creature find warmth and food. But they can also warn the animal away from heat that might dry out its skin.

The First Eyes

The next step in the evolution of the eye was an ability to detect motion. The third major step was the ability of the eye to form images.

3

How often do you say to a friend, "See what I mean?" or "Do you see?" It means, "Do you understand?" One of the best ways of remembering or understanding something is to make a picture of it in our minds. Part of what we do when we think is compare different images, or mind pictures. The

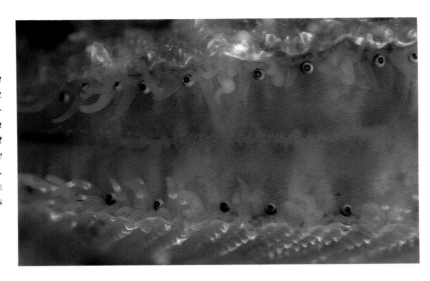

Arranged in rows, the rock scallop's single-lens eyes can detect movement but do not see objects clearly.
Jack Drafahl–IMAGE CONCEPTS

nerve cells of the eye and the brain are so similar that some vision scientists believe that the brain evolved as a result of primitive eyes trying to make sense of the images they received from the world around them.

Images and Light

It is important to realize that we do not see objects themselves, but only the light they reflect. *An image is a pattern of light.* The clearest images reveal the world in detailed patterns of light and dark. The most sensitive eyes can detect the slightest change in brightness, changes in light to dark, and dark to light.

All eyes have one major function in common—they are catchers of light. Each eye in your head contains about 180 million (180,000,000) tiny receptors or light catchers, called *photoreceptors* (**fo**-to-ree-**sep**-tors), which are ready to absorb equally small bits of light energy known as *photons* (fo-tons). Photons are bits of energy that bounce off objects into the eye. They are produced by the intense heat of our own sun and distant stars, or by fire or manmade electricity. As you read this page, millions of photons are streaming

4

into your eyes. Most of them will bounce out, but the bits of light energy (photons) that are absorbed by the photoreceptors in your eyes will be transformed into rich and apparently seamless images.

The word *retina* (**ret**-i-nah) means "little net" in Latin. Millions of photoreceptors cluster together in what might be described as a net or screen on which images are formed. In the vertebrate eye the curved outer *cornea* (**cornee-a**) and lens of the eye are designed to direct the flight of photons toward the photoreceptors of the retina.

Sunglasses for animals? If you don't have eyelids, how can you protect yourself against unwanted light? One answer may be to reflect or bounce back the light. The glittering eyes of this puffer fish and the horsefly are doing just that. Jack Drafahl–IMAGE CONCEPTS

There are two types of photoreceptors in the vertebrate eye: *rods* and *cones*. Rods work in dim light but shut down in bright light. Cones are activated by bright light and allow us to see in color. They turn off when light dims below a certain level. If you go from a very bright place to one that is dark, there are several moments when you can't see very well. Your eyes are unable to send visual information to the brain because the cones stop functioning and the rods take time to activate.

5

Seeing Near and Far   People and animals whose eyes are especially round are said to be *near-sighted*—able to see best up close. The photons in such eyes land in front of most of the retina's photoreceptors. The eyes of a *farsighted* person or animal are more flat and the photons land behind the great mass of photoreceptors, causing the eyes to focus best on far-off objects.

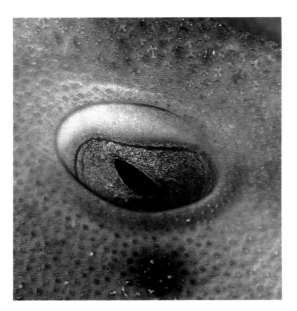 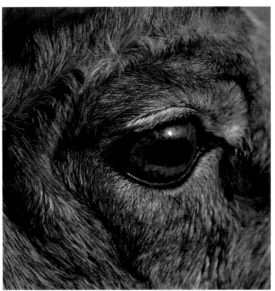

The pupils of animal eyes come in all sorts of shapes. But animals that must scan the horizon for predators often have horizontal pupils like the horn shark or the bighorn sheep shown here.
Sue Drafahl–IMAGE CONCEPTS/Len Rue, Jr.

Color Vision   Light travels from its source to the eye in a wavelike motion. Different colors have different wavelengths of light. To see in color, a person or animal's eyes must be able to recognize wavelengths of different sizes. An apple looks red to our eyes because photons, traveling on the long wavelengths that we see as red, bounce from the apple into our eyes, which absorb them. Tree leaves appear green to us for the same reason. The more sensitive an animal's eyes are to changes in the size of the wavelengths, the more colors that animal will see. The smaller, more energetic waves are seen as *ultraviolet* (**ul**-tra-vi-o-let) or blue in color. The larger, less energetic waves appear as red and even *infrared* (**in**-fra-red).

People cannot see either ultraviolet or infrared, although other creatures

6

can. What is called *visible light,* or light seen by the human eye, ranges in between ultraviolet and infrared. These colors can all be seen by passing white light through a glass prism. From the shortest wavelength to the longest wavelength they are: violet, indigo, blue, green, yellow, orange, and red. Between these basic colors are many variations like pink and turquoise. It is estimated that the trained human eye can make out as many as 150 different hues or shades of colors.

When people think of differences in the way that various animals see, they usually start with color. The leaves of a tree, for example, appear green or somewhat yellowish-green to our eyes, but to a flying insect or a pigeon flying above, those very same leaves might appear to be red or red-orange. A squirrel climbing through the branches of that tree would see the leaves as a sort of off-white, although if the leaves were yellow, they would see them as yellow because this is a wavelength they can absorb. To a raccoon or an owl these same leaves appear simply bright, with no color at all.

Animals See Colors Differently

Another major difference in how animals see is the number of images their eyes can make per second. Most of us assume the world is passing before our eyes just as it is. But the human eye can only make about sixty images a second in daylight and about ten images at night. These images appear so rapidly to our brain that our conscious minds are unaware of what's happening. But that speed is slow motion compared to the eyes of a flying insect, which processes as many as 360 images per second in daylight. The eyes of these insects can be thought of as high-speed cameras.

Images in Time

Of course, there are creatures whose eyes make only a very few images per second, like the lovely chambered nautilus. Once upon a time there were many millions of similar animal species. Few survive today, for they are preyed upon by creatures that they cannot see or sometimes see too late.

Our own eyes are placed squarely in the front of our heads. The fields of vision of the two eyes overlap, which helps us judge the distance between ourselves and another animal or to throw a baseball neatly into the glove of

Predator and Prey

a catcher. We share the ability to judge distance with other animals who, like ourselves, are *predators*, those who kill other animals for food. Lions, wolves, snakes, and sharks are examples of predators.

Sharks have little color vision, but unlike all modern bony fish, these great predators of the ocean tend to be farsighted. Carl Roessler–ANIMALS ANIMALS

Creatures of *prey*—those that are hunted by other animals, like the rabbit, squirrel, and duck—have eyes on the sides of their heads. This enables them to see what might be coming up from behind them. The only place where an animal's eye position does not distinguish a predator from its prey is underwater, where every creature seems to be at risk from another one.

Single-lens and Compound Eyes The eyes of most creatures on earth can be divided into two kinds: the single-lens eye such as our own, and the compound eye. The single-lens eye is found in animals that need to see well at a distance. It is the kind of eye that vertebrates have. The compound eye is the eye of animals that see well up close and is the eye that most invertebrates have. There are some invertebrates, however, such as the robber fly and the king crab, that have both single-lens and compound eyes.

8

3 ❧ Seeing Close Up

A compound eye would have to be huge—at least three feet wide—to be able to see as well as the human eye does at a distance. Our heads would have to be enormous for such eyes, and our skeletons could not lift such a heavy weight.

All insects have compound eyes, although some have single-lens eyes as well. Compound eyes are also found in crustaceans, of which the best known are shrimp, crabs, and lobsters. One similarity between crustaceans and insects is that both become temporarily blind when they shed their *exoskeletons* (ex-oh-skel-e-tons). The largest of all compound eyes is found in the lobster.

The design of modern telescopes owes much to the eyes of the lobster, which have a complex system of internal "mirrors" that help guide the creature across the dim ocean floor. Jack Drafahl– IMAGE CONCEPTS

The single-lens eye has only one lens, but compound eyes always have more than one, and these tiny lenses are referred to as *lenslets*. Primitive insects like centipedes or ladybugs have few lenslets (some only nine or ten), while flying insects like the bee and dragonfly have many, many thousands. In the compound eye there is no cornea, the clear, outer protective layer that single-lens eyes have, and the lenslets are located on the surface of the eye.

Flying insects such as the California red dragonfly are like fighter pilots and can capture their prey on the wing. Jack Drafahl–IMAGE CONCEPTS

Advantages of the Compound Eye The compound eye cannot change focus for near and far vision. Animals with compound eyes must move closer or farther away to see an object better. But creatures with compound eyes do have some advantages. For example, they can make out details in a twig or flower that would not be visible to our eyes without a microscope. As you bring your finger closer to your nose, you will see it go out of focus. But a creature with a compound eye can see an object clearly right next to its eye.

Another advantage of the compound eye is that it gets an equally clear picture from all directions, while the single-lens eye sees an area only as large as the tip of a thumb with perfect clarity. We are unaware of this limitation

10

because our eyes are constantly moving around. Try staring at one word on this page for a few seconds. You will soon become aware that the rest of the page is out of focus.

Scientists once thought that insects saw crude images, but they now know that flying insects see very well within their range. The reason has more to do with the size of their eyes' photoreceptors than with the quality of the compound lenslets. Despite the small size of the bee, for example, its photoreceptors are the same size as our own.

One of the most important characteristics of the photoreceptors or light-catchers of the compound eye, called *rhabdoms* (**rab**-dums), is that they face the incoming light. In comparison, the rods and cones of vertebrate animals have a harder task of capturing light since they face away from the incoming light toward the brain, and must capture photons as they bounce off the back of the eye.

Most flying insects see in color. The range of color vision of some butter-flies surpasses that of any other creature on earth. One explanation is that flying insects and flowering plants evolved at the very same time in earth's history.

One of the great mysteries in natural science is how some plants have evolved to look exactly like the insects they attract, like this bee orchid.
R. Johns–ANIMALS ANIMALS

11

4 ✖ Clusters of Eyes

Hunting and Weaving Spiders

Spiders can be divided into two groups: hunters and weavers. The weaver weaves a sticky web that entraps other insects, while the hunting spider must capture its prey. It should come as no surprise that the hunters have the better vision; in fact, hunters have two additional eyes, eight altogether, while weavers are limited to six.

Spiders have clusters of eyes that operate in pairs. The eyes on the sides of the spider's head detect motion. One pair in the front of the head judges distance, and another pair forms images. Our own single-lens eyes are able to perform all these functions.

While weavers do not see as well as the hunters, one of the more interesting questions in science is how some weavers are aware that other creatures see quite well. They weave patterns called *stabilamenta* (sta-bil-ah-**men**-ta) into their webs that are visible to larger creatures like birds that might otherwise damage the webs by flying through them. The stabilamenta warn the bird of the sticky web.

Weaving spiders don't see very well but somehow they know that other creatures do. They weave patterns called stabilamenta that warn larger animals like birds to stay away from the sticky web. Patti Murray–ANIMALS ANIMALS

12

The best vision of any hunting spider belongs to a class called jumping spiders because of their ability to leap great distances after their prey, one as much as twenty times its body size. Jumpers have excellent close-up vision. They can also see in color, though their vision is better toward the ultraviolet end of the spectrum. Spiders have fixed-focus lenses and see best only a few inches away from an object.

The jumping spider (left) *cannot spin, so must depend on keen eyesight and quick movements to hunt for its food. The female netcasting spider of Australia* (top right and bottom)—*the world's most unusual weaving spider—has such good eyesight that it is able to cast its net over unsuspecting victims. Other weaving spiders simply sit on their webs and wait for prey to appear.* Jack Drafahl–IMAGE CONCEPTS *(top left)*; Jim Frazier and Densey Clyne–MANTIS WILDLIFE FILMS *(top right and bottom)*.

13

5 ✖ The Underwater Eye

While most undersea creatures are fish, many other animals also live underwater: *cephalopods* (**sef**-allo-pods), a Greek word meaning head *(cephalo)* and foot *(pod)*, which include the octopus and squid; crustaceans like the crab and the lobster; deep-sea mammals such as seals, porpoises, and whales; as well as all sorts of simple marine invertebrates.

The struggle to survive underwater has always been fierce. While land animals can be separated into predator and prey by the position of their eyes, in the sea all animals are at risk and most have their eyes positioned on the sides to carefully watch out for what might be coming up behind them. Flatfish that live on the ocean floor, like the flounder or the ray, are exceptions.

All flatfish have eyes on the top of their heads. They are born with eyes at each side but like this flounder, one eye migrates toward the other side as the fish matures, and it spends the rest of its life staring upward. Joan Giannechini

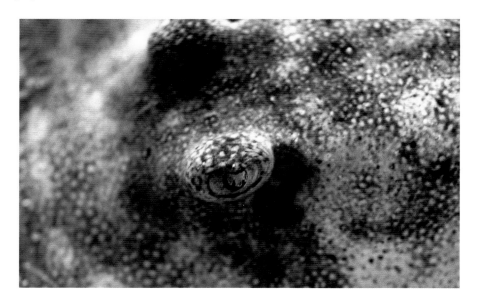

They are born with eyes on both sides of the head, but as they develop, one eye migrates to the other side and they spend their mature lives looking upward.

All underwater animals must cope with the same problem. As photons of *Underwater* light pass through water, they strike individual molecules of water, scattering *Light* in all directions. The effect of this on the eye (to the human eye as well) is glare.

Water acts as a light filter. The deeper we descend into the ocean, the fewer colors can be seen. After the first fifty feet below the water's surface all ultra-violet and infrared wavelengths of light are blocked. As we go further down, only blue-green wavelengths of light can penetrate the water for any distance. This means that fish in deeper waters see colors toward the blue end of the spectrum. A diver who bleeds underwater will see his blood as green instead of red. All fish in deep water appear to be bluish-gray, but when pulled to the surface may be red. Below 1500 feet no light penetrates and the sea is a perpetual night.

Land animals can separate an object from its background by its brightness. *Color Vision* Underwater, only an object's color sets it apart. This may be one of the rea- *in Fish* sons why color vision is widespread among the most advanced fish, the bony fish that dominate the waters of the world. The bony fish, as you might guess, have interior skeletons and are vertebrates like ourselves.

The eyes of modern bony fish like this grouper are very round and tend to be near-sighted. Joan Giannechini

15

Primitive fish that have been around in their present form for millions of years like the *elasmobranch* (e-**laz**-mo-branch), which includes sharks, eels, and rays, have little or no color vision. Their internal skeletons are composed of cartilage (elastic tissue such as that found in the end of one's nose) rather than bone, and have eyes with few, if any, color photoreceptors.

The Fish Eye What is most unusual about a fish's eye is that it has no lids; fish sleep with their eyes open. Fish also lack pupils that control the amount of light entering the eye, by opening wider or growing smaller. We describe an event as occurring in the blink of an eye. That's how fast we can protect our own eyes by closing them. But the fish eye can only protect its sensitive eyes from bright light by covering them with a colored pigment found in the photoreceptors. It takes a long time for the pigment to surround the photoreceptors, and fish that live in the depths tend to rise to the surface of the water to feed very slowly. Anyone who keeps a fish tank should take care never to abruptly turn on the tank's light in the dark. The experience can be a painful one for the fish.

The Intelligent Octopus and Squid Much of what we know about visual memory comes from a long study of the octopus in the Mediterranean Sea. Octopi have giant *neurons* (new-rons)— the cells that link the central nervous system to the brain. Because of their

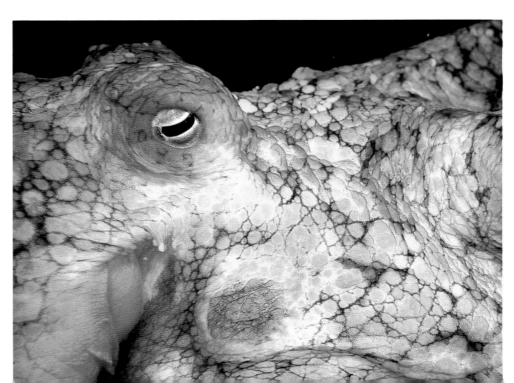

The octopus has a horizontal pupil that allows it to scan the watery horizon for predators.
Jack Drafahl– IMAGE CONCEPTS

16

size they are easier to study than our own microscopic neurons, yet they function much the same way as ours do. Giant squids, which can range up to more than fifty feet in length, have the largest eyes of any living animal.

What is unusual about each eye of the cephalopod is that it looks like a single-lens eye with a horizontal pupil. But the interior of the eye functions just like the compound eye of other invertebrates such as crustaceans and insects. The vision of cephalopods is somewhat cruder than our own. From experiments we know that they can only recognize a solid shape, not an outline.

Whales and porpoises were once land animals but returned to the sea some *Underwater* sixty-five million years ago. Seals and walruses followed a few million years *Mammals* later. Baby seals in the womb have their eyes positioned in front of their heads, like any land predator. But by the time they are born, the eyes have moved off to the sides, giving them a wider field of vision.

Like all deep-sea mammals, the eyes of the walrus are spaced wide apart for maximum range of vision. Jack Drafahl–IMAGE CONCEPTS

The eyes of whales are so widely separated that they have an enormous blind spot for any object directly in front of them. Whalers knew this and when they hunted, would steer their boats straight at the whale.

Below 1,500 feet in the ocean it is a miracle that animals can see at all. Without *bioluminescence* (by-oh-loo-mih-**ness**-ence), which is light created by living organisms (*bio* comes from the Greek word for life, and *lumen* comes from the Latin, meaning light), most deep-sea creatures would be blind. They either make their own light or use the light made by others. Many fish carry bioluminescent bacteria in their bodies. The flashlight fish of the Red Sea carries such bacteria in its eyes and can make them luminous by adding or removing oxygen. One deep-sea fish has a flap of skin coated with bioluminescent bacteria hanging over its mouth. A fish that grabs at the flap soon

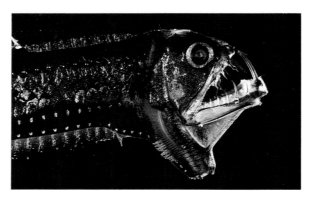

Bioluminescent bacteria in the skin of the chauliodus, a glow fish, casts an eerie light in the ocean depths. Oxford Scientific Films— Animals Animals

becomes the bioluminescent one's meal. Charles William Beebe, the first man to descend into the ocean depths in a steel diving tank called a *bathysphere*, compared bioluminescent light to stars at night.

Bioluminescent light is unlike all other forms of illumination because, although it gives off a great deal of light, it is cold, not hot, to the touch. Bioluminescent light is 90% light and only 10% heat. While bioluminescent creatures are found on land and in the salty seas, they are not found in clear streams, lakes, or rivers.

6 ❧ The First Land Eye—Amphibians

Amphibians (am-**fib**-ee-ans) are animals that are born in water but spend their adult life on land, though they must return to water to breed. They were the first animals to emerge onto dry land and are believed to have descended from an ancient group of fish with the long name of *crossoptery-gian* (cross-op-te-**ridge**-ee-an) that are now extinct. The eyes of the crossop-terygian provide the basic clue: They had a survival adaptation that is not found in modern bony fish—pupils that could open wider in dim light or get smaller to block out excessive light. Only a creature that could control the amount of light entering its eyes could survive on land. Imagine an amphibian without pupils, out and about on a foggy day. If the sun suddenly comes out, an overflow of electrical signals would be sent on to the brain. The creature would be in great pain and stunned—unable to move—and at the mercy of predators. A similar process occurs when an electrical appliance receives a sudden overcharge of electricity—it burns out.

Pupils were one form of protection for amphibians against sudden, bright light. As time went on, they evolved eyelids, folds of skin that open and close quickly. Eyelids also prevent dust and debris from entering the eye. Some amphibians have both upper and lower eyelids. The upper lid activates the tear gland, while the lower lid spreads an oily substance over the eye. Amphibians were the first creatures with eyes that produce tears. These tears, like our own, are salty, a reminder that both our ancestors once lived in ancient seas.

The bright coloring of some poisonous animals such as this red and black poison arrow frog warns enemies away. Zig Leszczynski–ANIMALS ANIMALS

When amphibians are born, their eyes are sphere-shaped like those of fish, designed for vision in water. By the time they reach adulthood, the lens has flattened out, improving their distance vision. This may be for only a few feet, but it makes it possible for a frog or toad to capture a flying insect that happens to hover within range.

A Thinking Eye   In primitive creatures with tiny brains the eye is sometimes described as a "thinking eye." That is, decisions are made based on reactions in the eye, rather than the brain.

The frog has the most interesting eye of all amphibians. What is extraordinary about this eye is its ability to detect movement. There are some vision scientists who believe that frogs cannot see an object if it does not move.

This wood frog, like all frogs, has distinctively shaped pupils and can be recognized by these alone. Jack Drafahl–IMAGE CONCEPTS

Much of the frog's behavior is based on choices made by the eye alone, rather than eye and brain together. This enables a frog to respond more quickly and attempt to catch almost anything that comes into its "snapping range," an area of several feet around its body.

20

Its small brain does play a role in visual memory, in that the frog can remember the shape and coloring of objects or creatures that have caused it pain, such as a bee or wasp, and avoid them. Frogs also have some color vision and respond positively to blues and blue-greens.

Although brightly colored, the red-eyed tree frog is not poisonous. Zig Leszczynski–ANIMALS ANIMALS

All amphibians have one real advantage over more advanced animals: They are able to *regenerate* (that is, grow again) portions of their body that have been damaged or destroyed. A newt can regenerate an eye in a year's time; a frog can repair a cut optic (eye) nerve in several months. Human beings pay a price for the complexity and specialization of their organs; the ability to repair is, in comparison, very limited.

7 ❧ Cold-Blooded Eyes—Reptiles

the giant dinosaurs. We can tell something
nt creatures since we know that like present-
led and not usually active when the sun
eyes had to function in bright light and it
were primarily cones (photoreceptors that
e of most reptiles. Only turtles—the most
vith all cones. The eyes of lizards such as
mposed of rod photoreceptors, and their
ost snakes have a combination of rod and

Errata
The paragraph on page 22 should read:

The oldest living reptiles, turtles and crocodilians
(which include both alligators and crocodiles) existed
when the giant dinosaurs dominated life on earth. If
dinosaurs were cold-blooded and not usually active
when the sun went down, their eyes would have had to
function in bright light and it is likely that their photoreceptors were primarily cones (photoreceptors that
work only in bright light). Of the reptiles only turtles
—the most ancient living reptiles—have eyes with all
cones. The eyes of lizards such as the alligator and
crocodile are composed of rod photoreceptors, and
their eyes function best in dim light. Most snakes have
a combination of rod and cone vision.

*Crocodiles are the most primitive creatures to care for their offspring. Their eyes see best in dim
light but they have stenopeic pupils like the gecko, which enable them to function in daylight.*
Jack and Sue Drafahl—IMAGE CONCEPTS

Reptiles were the first creatures to be able to follow an object with their eyes while keeping their heads still. The African chameleon carries this mobility to extremes. Its two eyes can look in two directions at once: front and back, up and down, and to either side at the same time.

The eyes of this African chameleon can look in two directions at once—up and down or to either side. Joan Giannechini

Crocodiles and alligators have eyes that function best at night, but these creatures are often awake in the daytime. Rod photoreceptors simply turn off in bright light. If the animals are to see during the day, they must be able to limit the amount of light entering the eyes so that their rods continue to work.

The circular pupil, in animals with eyes such as our own, closes down and gets smaller in bright light, as does the slit pupil found in the cat and many snakes—but not small enough to protect the eye. Crocodiles and alligators developed an even more effective light-blocker, the *stenopeic* (sten-o-**pay**-ic)

Blocking Out Light— The Stenopeic Pupil

23

pupil. When the stenopeic pupil gets very small, it shuts down to two extremely tiny holes, the size of pinheads. This type of pupil is also found in sea snakes and seals, as well as in nocturnal lizards. Most of these creatures spend a good deal of their time swimming in or on top of the water, where the glare from sunlight can be intense. The stenopeic pupil enables the animal to strictly control the amount of light entering the eye.

The gecko's eye has the best light-blocking pupil of all, the stenopeic pupil, which in bright light shuts down to two tiny holes the size of pinpricks. Zig Leszczynski–Animals Animals

If you take photographs, you know that the smaller the opening of your lens, the greater the distance over which you will have a sharp picture. This is called "depth of field." Similarly, animals with stenopeic pupils see a very sharp image over a large area, despite the small amount of light entering the eye.

Snakes' Eyes   Snakes cannot cry. They are the only reptile without tear glands. In addition, over a long period of time, their eyelids have fused to form a clear covering called a *spectacle,* which can become scratched. One venturesome vision scientist is reported to have polished the spectacle of a large python and observed that the snake appeared distinctly grateful.

The structure of an eye can tell you fascinating things about an animal. For example, we know that both the ancestors of mammals as well as the ancestors of modern snakes experienced a period during which they became nocturnal. We also know that both kinds of animals returned to life in the sunlight at about the same time in earth's history, because the eyes of mammals and snakes began to use a new method of blocking out ultraviolet light. Both eyes have two yellow filters, one in the lens and another one in front of the major concentration of cone receptors.

Why does the eye block out light? The job of a developed eye is to give the animal a clear picture of its world. But with possibly one exception, the butterfly, no eye can make both the very short wavelengths (ultraviolet) and the very long wavelengths (infrared and reds) land in the right place on the retinal screen. If all wavelengths got through, the result would be a blurred image. The evolutionary solution was to sacrifice some color vision. One of the general rules in vision science is that eyes block either ultraviolet light or reds and infrareds. For example, snakes and people can't see ultraviolet colors while bees, which can distinguish ultraviolet, cannot see red colors.

Most snakes are diurnal, or active during daylight, and have very good color vision. The best vision of all diurnal snakes is that of the cobra. When it weaves back and forth, it is just trying to get something or someone in better focus before it strikes. Nocturnal snakes, which are active at night, have slit pupils, like the cat. And sea snakes have the stenopeic pupil of crocodiles, geckoes, and seals.

In addition to their normal eyes, snakes of the *boid* (bo-id) family and pit vipers, including water moccasins, copperheads, and rattlesnakes, have infrared sensors, generally located around the snake's mouth, and can "see" in pitch dark if the object that they're looking at gives off heat. A photograph of a mouse taken with a thermographic camera, a fairly recent invention, gives an idea of what these snakes see in the dark. This camera makes pictures from heat radiation rather than light.

Images From Heat

25

Rattlesnakes have special heat-sensing ducts below their eyes that allow them to make images out of heat radiation and thus to "see" in pitch darkness. In daylight an opossum would appear to a rattlesnake more or less as we would see it. The color picture of the small rodent taken with a heat-sensitive thermographic camera shows how a snake would see an opossum at night. Leonard Lee Rue III *(snake)*/Jack Drafahl—ANIMALS ANIMALS *(opossum)*/S. L. Craig, Jr. *(thermographic photo)*

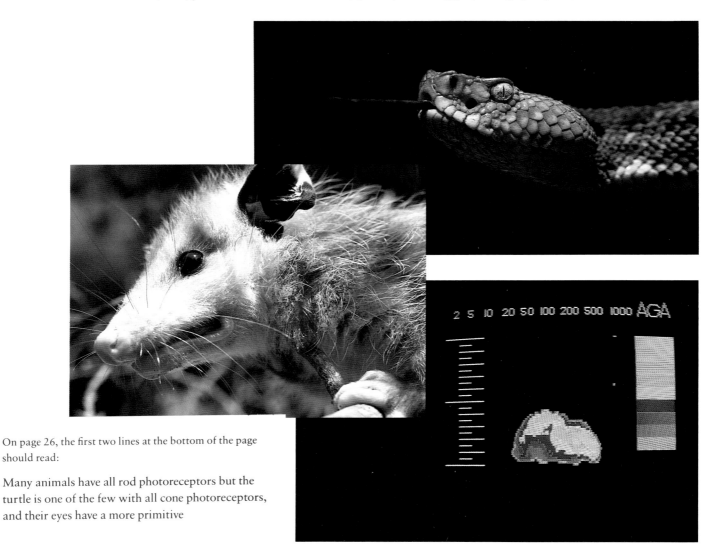

2 5 10 20 50 100 200 500 1000 AGA

On page 26, the first two lines at the bottom of the page should read:

Many animals have all rod photoreceptors but the turtle is one of the few with all cone photoreceptors, and their eyes have a more primitive

Turtles— Oil Droplet Filters Turtles are a much older species than snakes. Like their dinosaur ancestors, they have only cone photoreceptors, and their eyes have a more primitive way of filtering out light that they share with fish, birds, lizards, amphibians, and insects. Turtle eyes block out unwanted wavelengths of light with colored oil droplets found in the individual photoreceptors.

While the yellow filters in snakes and mammals simply block out all ultra-violet light (or colors), oil droplet filters can vary in color, and creatures with oil droplet filters can have a greater sensitivity to changes in hues or shades of color.

The eyes of all sea turtles, like this hawksbill turtle, are filled with tiny red filters. We would see these reef fish as yellow, but to a turtle they would appear reddish. Sue Drafahl–IMAGE CONCEPTS

But the oil droplets in turtle eyes are predominantly red. In cameras, red filters improve contrast and this is also true for the eye. Red filters darken objects that are dark and as a result, light objects stand out. Sea turtles, which are great travelers, may need greater contrast because they navigate through the world's oceans. It is interesting to note that red oil droplets are also found in sea birds and pigeons that are navigators of the skies.

8 ✒ Flying Eyes

Long-Distance Vision

Birds have the best distance vision of any creature on earth, and no animal sees farther better than predatory birds such as the hawk or eagle. Hawks can see us from the air when we don't even know they're flying above us. But the eyes of birds have developed at the expense of the brain in that they have become so large, they've left little room in the skull for the brain to develop.

Look sharp! The hawk sees best at a distance—about eight times farther than the human eye can see.
Zig Leszczynski–
ANIMALS ANIMALS

Only in birds and mammals (and not all) do we find eyes that see well both near and far. We can look at the lines in the palms of our hands, and in a twinkling change focus, and clearly see a distant star. Muscles in the eye squeeze the lens and change its shape to suit near or far vision. But predatory birds like the hawk and eagle have an additional set of muscles that change the shape of the outer cornea as well. This improves their distance vision, and a hawk can see clearly approximately eight times farther than a person can.

Iridescent colors are not real colors at all but the effects of wavelengths of light passing through transparent layers, like the feathers of this hummingbird. Some of the light waves (or colors) are so strongly reinforced that the birds appear to glitter with color. But if the feathers were pressed together, we would see that they are a dull gray. Leonard Lee Rue III

29

Upper and Lower Eyelids Birds have both upper and lower eyelids. The bottom lid sweeps the cornea like a windshield wiper. Birds also have a see-through skin covering called a *nictitating membrane* that shields nocturnal birds from excessive light during the day. Seabirds who often fly for days at a time use it to shield their eyes from flying debris.

The Owl The owl is the best known of all nocturnal birds. It is one of the very few birds with a fixed-focus lens, a lens that lacks the muscles to change focus for near and far vision. Owls must lean far back to focus on food in front of them—only then can they grab it with their beak. The eyes of the owl are enormously large, and like those of deep-sea fish, they have become tubular in shape and fill almost the entire skull.

The great horned owl's nocturnal eye has a nictitating membrane that blocks out light during the day. Jack Drafahl–IMAGE CONCEPTS

30

Vision scientists have always been fascinated by the ability of pigeons to recognize pictures more quickly than people can. Here is another example of what might be called a thinking eye. The pigeon's eyes are "coded" for designs or patterns like those of pictures. This ability assists pigeons in recognizing familiar terrain and is, no doubt, one of the reasons why they have been used as messenger birds throughout recorded history.

9 ❧ The Dark-Adapted Eye

The stars do not come out at night. They are always there, but our eyes require the contrast of the dark night sky for us to see them. For millions of years the only light available for vision at night was the reflected light of the moon and starlight. In order to be able to see at all, the rod photoreceptors of nocturnal animals pool the photons that enter the eye from many different directions. Since so many images are overlaid, one on top of the other, only what is very bright stands out. As a result nocturnal animals live in a world of crude shapes and outlines with little texture or detail.

Since color vision is almost unknown among nocturnal animals, they distinguish one object from another by its relative brightness. Plants that are pollinated by night creatures like bats and moths are generally white. What is curious is how nocturnal animals perceive brightness. For example, we see yellow as the brightest color, but to the nocturnal animal it is green. A fruit bat thinks a banana is darker than its green leaf. A raccoon spotting a buttercup sees the green leaves more brightly than the yellow flower. Their eyes are simply unable to process anything brighter than green, so yellows, oranges, and reds appear dark.

Most of the light that enters an eye bounces out. Inside the eyes of nocturnal animals are reflecting mirrors called *tapeta* (tah-**pi**-tah), the Latin plural for tapetum. These mirrors are designed to bounce or reflect photons back toward the retina that might otherwise have bounced out of the eye. When light strikes the eyes of a dog or cat, their eyes seem to glow in the dark. This is the light reflected by the tapeta shining back. Tapeta are found in all sorts of nocturnal animals as well as deep-sea fish.

The strange glow of a timber wolf's eyes is caused by light reflecting from the tapeta.
E. R. Degginger–
ANIMALS ANIMALS

The Bat The bat is the only flying mammal. For a long time it was thought to have poor vision. The explanation for its ability to find its way in the dark was *echolocation* (ek-oh-low-**ka**-shun). Bats emit a series of clicking sounds that bounce off objects and insects or animals. The returning signal tells bats the object's or animal's location. Recent tests, however, have shown that blind-folded bats lose their way, which supports the idea that they do need their eyes to guide them. Researchers have also learned that some bats find fish by watching ripples in the water.

32

Batting an eye: The nocturnal bat—here, an Australian fruit bat—does not need to see in color. While to humans an orchid is very colorful, a bat only sees shades of bright and dark. Hans and Judy Beste—Animals Animals *(bat)*/Jack and Sue Drafahl—Image Concepts *(orchid, color and black and white)*

Primates are the most highly developed order of mammals and include man, lemurs, apes, and monkeys. The earliest primates were all nocturnal. Some of them, like the tarsier of Southeast Asia or the douracouli monkey of South America still are. In proportion to its body the tarsier has the largest eyes of any living creature—150 times bigger, in relation to its body, than the human eye. In fact, they are so large that the tarsier cannot move them in their sockets but has to twist its head to follow a moving object. It can literally turn and look directly over its own shoulder, an ability it shares with the nocturnal owl whose eyes are also too large to move.

The tarsier's eyes are so large that it cannot move them in the eye sockets. To follow a moving object it must turn its head. Like the owl, it can literally turn its head around and look over its own shoulder. Densey Clyne–Mantis Wildlife Films

The eyes of the nocturnal douracouli monkey are so delicate that this animal can go blind if exposed to bright light. Michael Dick–BRUCE COLEMAN INC.

10 ❧ Eye and Brain

Paw, Claw, Hoof, and Hand

What do a paw or a claw or a hoof or a hand have to do with the way a creature sees? Once the dinosaurs disappeared, the mammals that had fled to the darkness for safety began to re-enter the daylight. Animals that came down from the trees had a real advantage. In addition to having developed a hand for grasping, they now had muscles that could change the shape of the lens in their eyes for near and far vision.

But mammals with paws, claws, or hooves did not develop this muscular system. (There is one known exception: the river otter. This otter is a master builder and constantly uses its paws to grasp twigs and other items it uses for construction.) Mammals with claws and paws generally have fixed lenses. Few diurnal mammals are nearsighted, unlike human beings. In fact, many are farsighted, like the gazelle and other animals of the plains. This is obviously a survival mechanism at work since they are constantly scanning the horizon for predators.

Like all animals with paws and claws, this Alaskan brown bear has eyes that cannot change focus for near and far vision. Tom Edwards— ANIMALS ANIMALS

Some vision scientists believe that the horse uses different parts of its retina for near and far vision. The upper part of the retina is used for far vision while the lower portion is for seeing well up close. Robert Maier— ANIMALS ANIMALS

Color Vision in Mammals It is only among the great apes, monkeys, and humans that we find color vision that comes close to that of birds. Red-green blindness (the inability to distinguish reds or greens) is a rare disease in human beings, but it is the way

36

many mammals see. These animals see yellows and blues the way we do, but greens appear as sort of an off-white and reds simply go dark. This is normal vision for prairie dogs and squirrels. The receptors of the eye that distinguish these two color areas are the last to develop.

Cats see color far better than dogs do, but their best color vision is very pale, almost pastellike. They have so few color receptors (cones) that in order to see in daylight, their vast number of rods must work with their limited number of cones. They keep their rod photoreceptors from shutting down by narrowing their slit pupils so that very little light can enter the eye. But since the color signal of the cone mixes with brightness information (black or white) from their rods, the color signal is weakened.

Color vision varies widely among mammals. Pouched animals, or *marsupials* (mar-**soo**-pee-als), have no known color vision and all have fixed-focus lenses. Deer have few cone receptors. Hippos and elephants have so few photoreceptors that they are reputed to see clearly for only several hundred feet and do not see in color. The giraffe has been tested for color vision and it seems to be able to recognize reds and violets, though it confuses green, orange, and yellow.

The color vision of the great apes of Africa comes closest to resembling our own. The color vision of the African green monkey and the macaque also closely matches ours. South American primates are less developed and most South American monkeys can barely distinguish reds.

The primate brain, especially the human brain, not only stores visual information, it actually plays an important role in transforming the nature of the visual image itself. For example, the brain improves color vision in some primates and most humans. As the descendants of creatures that lived in leafy trees, we naturally see green and yellow-green best. But the brain cancels out some of the green information and deliberately sends red, a weaker color signal, to its visual centers. The brain has become so important to vision that if the visual centers of a primate brain are destroyed, that animal will be blind even if its eyes are in excellent condition. This is not true of more primitive creatures like amphibians or fish.

The Primate Brain and Vision

The vision of African monkeys most resembles our own. They see color very much the way that we do. Phil Savoie–BRUCE COLEMAN INC.

Depth Vision   The brain improves the ability of animals to judge distance. All animal brains have two lobes, or sides: a left lobe and a right lobe. Because eyes are set apart, each one sees an image slightly differently. In all animals *except* mammals, what one eye sees goes only to the opposite side of the brain. In mammals at least *some* of the visual information is sent to *both* sides of the brain. The mammal's brain can then compare the two images. This sharing of visual information by the two lobes of the brain enables mammals to judge the distance between themselves and an object, and to coordinate the movements of the eye; the pupils of each eye now get larger or smaller together.

Once the brain could compare two images, the next step in the evolution

38

of vision became possible. Only humans and the great apes see the world in *stereoscopic* (stair-ee-oh-scop-ik), or three-dimensional, vision. This is because in the primate each eye sends an *equal* amount of information to both lobes of the brain. The bird, on the other hand, does not have stereoscopic vision. Despite its magnificent eyes, it can only use visual clues such as differences in size, position, distance, and so on, to figure out the location of an object.

The babies of primates, however, are not born with three-dimensional vision. After birth the primate brain grows larger, incredibly larger in the human child, and with it develops the brain centers that judge depth. (A person born blind, who gains vision after early childhood, will never develop these visual centers.) In addition, the visual centers of primate brains not only compare images seen in the present, but have the ability to store information and provide a constant flow of feedback comparing what has been seen before with what is new.

All brains have the ability to store visual memory so that the animal can compare past experience with new information. But the primate brain, in particular the human brain, has a vast visual memory bank that can be accessed with remarkable speed. It is no wonder that the primate came to dominate life on this earth.

Despite our superior brains, we can still learn a great deal from studying the eyes of animals. Studies of snakes have taught us how to make images out of heat rather than light, while the firefly has helped us discover how to make light from elements found in living tissue. The design of telescopes that search the sky for distant points of light has improved from the study of the compound eye of the lobster, which must find its way in the dim light of the sea. The eye of the frog, coded for movement, has helped in the design of the electric eye that automatically opens doors for us. Visual images of other creatures show us new ways—sometimes useful, even astounding—of understanding our world.

Index 🦋

About the Author

Sandra Sinclair is the author of *How Animals See: Other Visions of Our World,* as well as a number of articles on natural science. She has worked internationally as a producer and director of television commercials and films, and is president of Longmoor Productions, a film company located in New York City. Ms. Sinclair selected the photographs, made by world-famous nature photographers, for use in this book.